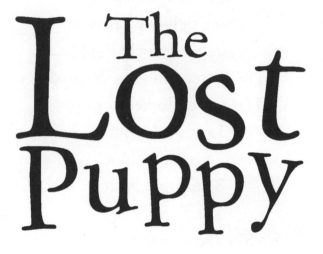

The Lost Puppy

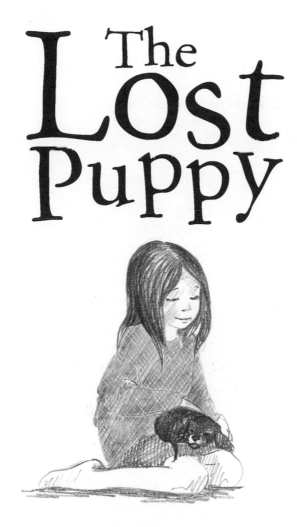

by Holly Webb

Illustrated by Sophy Williams

For Max, and for Georgie Dog

tiger tales

5 River Road, Suite 128, Wilton, CT 06897
Published in the United States 2016
Originally published in Great Britain 2012
by Little Tiger Press
Text copyright © 2012 Holly Webb
Illustrations copyright © 2012 Sophy Williams
ISBN-13: 978-1-58925-491-6
ISBN-10: 1-58925-491-0
Printed in China
STP/1800/0092/0216
All rights reserved
10 9 8 7 6 5 4 3 2 1

For more insight and activities, visit us at www.tigertalesbooks.com

Chapter One

"Christy! Happy Birthday!" Aunt Nell rushed down the path to hug Christy, with Maisy the dachshund galloping after her.

"Thanks, Aunt Nell!" Christy replied with a smile. "Hey, Maisy, where are the puppies?" she asked. Ever since Maisy had her puppies, she'd been curled up in her pen in the kitchen with them, as though she didn't dare let them out of her sight.

Aunt Nell shook her head. "I think she's getting a bit annoyed with them now that they're so much bigger. They spend all their time climbing over her, and nipping each other's ears, or Maisy's. They can't get over the board we've got across the kitchen door, but their mom can, and she's left them behind to get a break."

"Can we go and see them?" Christy asked. She'd always loved playing with Maisy, but the puppies were even more beautiful than their mom, and she hadn't seen them for a week. She was sure they'd have changed. They were 11 weeks old now, but they still seemed to be growing so fast that she could almost see it happening.

"Puppies!" Christy's three-year-old sister, Anna, demanded, stomping up the path. She loved the puppies as much as Christy did. Christy actually wondered if sometimes Anna thought she *was* a puppy. She curled up in their basket almost every time they came to visit Aunt Nell. Once she'd even tried their puppy food, but luckily she hadn't liked it.

"And hello to you too, Anna." Aunt Nell grinned as Anna hurried past her into the house. Christy chased after her little sister—if she wasn't quick, she'd probably find Anna sitting in the water bowl.

"So are you having a good birthday?" Aunt Nell asked. "Does it feel odd that you've already had your party?" Christy had shared her birthday party with her best friend, Beth, the previous weekend. Beth was two weeks older than Christy, so they'd split the difference.

"No, it's great!" Christy beamed at her. "It feels like I'm having two birthdays!"

"Well, I've got a present for you in the house." Aunt Nell had a curious smile on her face, Christy realized. She started to feel excited about the present.

She looked at her mom and dad, wondering if they knew what it was. Mom had exactly the same expression on her face as Aunt Nell, which Christy supposed wasn't that strange, since they were sisters.

"What is it?" she asked curiously.

"Why don't you come and see the puppies before you open your present?" Aunt Nell suggested. "Otherwise we'll find them all nibbling Anna's toes. It's almost their lunchtime."

The puppies were still having lots of small meals. "Is it oatmeal?" Christy asked hopefully, as they went into the kitchen. The last time they'd visited, the puppies had eaten milky oatmeal, and all of them had dangled their big ears in the bowl—and had come out with oatmeal-crusted ears afterward. It was really funny!

Aunt Nell laughed. "No, sorry, it's just biscuits. Very boring. But they like them. Now that they're old enough for their new homes, I'm weaning them off the milky stuff."

"Are they really big enough to leave Maisy?" Christy asked, peering around the kitchen door at the seething mass of brown and black puppies wriggling around in their pen. Maisy hopped elegantly over the board in the doorway, and headed back to her babies. The puppies saw her coming and flung themselves out of the pen, then scampered across the floor to their mom. Christy giggled. She was sure that she saw Maisy duck her head and dig her paws in as she was hit by a wave of puppies.

Aunt Nell nodded. "A couple of people have come to see them already."

"Six babies," Christy said to Dad, as she crouched down to get closer to the pups. "You always say Anna and I are enough!"

Dad nodded. "Quite enough!"

"I think she'll miss them when they're gone," Aunt Nell said. "But right now I don't think she's going to mind *that* much. And I am keeping one puppy."

"Oh, which one?" Christy asked, crossing her fingers behind her back.

"The little black girl puppy. I'm calling her Maggie. She gets along well with Maisy, I think. And I like that the names both begin with M."

Christy nodded, a little sadly. She had been hoping that Aunt Nell would keep her favorite puppy, the handsome boy with the black back and orange paws. He'd spotted her coming in, and now he trotted over to her eagerly. In her head, she'd named him Lucky, although she hadn't told anyone.

There was no point in naming him, really, since he would be going off to live somewhere else very soon. But Christy hadn't been able to help it. Lucky was just the perfect name for him.

He was such a funny little dog, always bouncing around. Christy rolled a jingly ball across the kitchen floor for him, and he skidded after it eagerly, his paws slipping around on the tiles. He was dashing after it so fast that he overshot, and had to screech to a halt and snatch it out of Maggie's paws. His sister growled at him angrily, then stomped away.

Lucky picked up the ball in his sharp little teeth, and marched triumphantly back to Christy, his ears swinging. Then he dropped it at her feet, wagging his tail and nosing it toward her, asking her to do it again.

Christy stroked his glossy fur. "Oh, you're so beautiful."

Anna, who had been lying on the kitchen floor to be on the same level as the puppies, wriggled her way over to Christy and Lucky, and nuzzled him, nose to nose. Lucky looked slightly shocked, but he nuzzled her, too, and then licked her generously on one cheek.

Anna squealed with delight and was about to lick him back when Mom grabbed her. "No licking the puppies!"

Mom glanced worriedly at Dad, but he was laughing.

"It'll be fine," he told her.

Christy frowned at them. What did

they mean? She was sure Lucky licking Anna just once wouldn't do her any harm.

"Why don't you pick him up?" Aunt Nell suggested. "He won't mind."

Christy gently slipped her hands under Lucky's smooth tummy, and snuggled him against her. He had climbed into her lap before, but she had never actually picked him up. He was so good to cuddle. She sighed quietly as she rubbed her cheek against his warm head, wondering if this was the last time she would see him.

Lucky sighed, too, but happily. He dug his nose under the shoulder of Christy's sweater, which made her giggle and squirm, then he scratched his claws against the fabric lovingly.

Aunt Nell smiled at her. "So, do you like your present?"

Christy looked up, confused.

Dad laughed, and Mom smiled at her, then eyed Lucky meaningfully.

"Lucky? The puppy, I mean?" Christy stared at them all, her mouth falling open in surprise.

"I told you she'd already named him!" Aunt Nell said. "He's always been the one Christy liked best. A lady wanted to choose him yesterday, Christy, but I told her he was reserved for you!"

"You're giving me Lucky for my

birthday?" Christy sounded dazed. "Can we take him home?" she added hopefully. "Or is he mine but at your house?" Mom and Dad had always said no to a dog, because Anna was too young. She looked up at them uncertainly. "You said not while Anna was little…."

"But he's not going to get big enough to knock Anna over," Dad pointed out. Lucky was a miniature dachshund—he'd never be bigger than about a foot tall. "And yes, he's coming home with us. Mom and I have decided you're both old enough now. He'll be yours mostly, Christy, but Anna's allowed to cuddle him, too, okay?"

Christy nodded. She didn't mind sharing at all. She was still shocked that they were actually getting their own dog! "Are we taking him home *today*?" she asked Aunt Nell.

"Absolutely. But you have to eat lunch first. And I made you another birthday cake!"

"Oh, wow! Oh, I have to call Beth and tell her we're really getting a dog!" Christy exclaimed. But then she looked worried. "Don't we need stuff? A basket … and bowls … and … lots of things…."

Aunt Nell held up one finger. "Just a minute." She disappeared into the garage and came back out with a huge cardboard box. "One perfect puppy package. This is your present from me, Christy. Lucky is from your mom and dad, so I said I would give you all the things you'd need to take care of him properly." She put the box down in front of Christy. "It's heavy!"

Lucky wriggled in Christy's arms, curious to see what was in such a huge box. Christy laughed. "I think you and Anna are going to be fighting over it," she told him. "Anna loves boxes." She hugged Lucky gently. It was still hard to believe he was really hers!

Chapter Two

Lucky traveled the 20-minute journey to Christy's house in a special cardboard box with flaps and a handle on top, which Aunt Nell had given them. But Mom had said that Christy could get him out as soon as the car pulled up at the house.

When Christy opened the flaps, Lucky was squashed into the corner of the box with his special blanket in his teeth, looking very worried. He really didn't understand what was happening, and he didn't like being jostled around. The box smelled strange, too. He was glad he had the blanket, which smelled of home, and the other puppies, and his mom. But he dropped it when he saw Christy and wagged his tail, just a little. He didn't move out of his corner, though.

"Hey, Lucky...," Christy whispered. "Are you okay? Was it scary being in the car?"

Lucky edged closer to her and stood with his front paws on the side of the box, looking up at her hopefully. He didn't like it in here. He wanted to be petted and held. And fed. He was starving.

Christy laughed as she picked him up and he nibbled at her jacket. "Are you hungry? Aunt Nell didn't want to feed you before we drove home—she said you might get sick. And she thought it would be good to feed you here. Then you'll have good first memories of being with us. In your new home!"

Lucky barked—a sharp, demanding "Feed me!" bark. He was sure he knew what Christy was talking about. Aunt Nell always talked to the puppies. *Should we feed you now, hmm?* That was what she said when she was getting the yummy biscuits out.

"Come on, then!" Christy followed Mom inside, and Dad staggered after them with the huge box, while Anna danced around them, singing a little dog-song she'd made up.

"We need to unpack, and then you'll get your dinner," Christy explained to Lucky, as she put him down gently on the kitchen floor. "Your bowls are in here, and a big bag of the food you like."

But Lucky was distracted from food for a moment, as he looked around the kitchen. Dad quickly closed the door. "We've got to keep him in here for a few days, remember," he told Christy. "Aunt Nell said to get him used to one room first."

"And there are tiles in here," Mom added. "So cleaning up will be easy if he makes any puddles. I know Aunt Nell started house-training him, but he's sure to be a little confused, and he might forget that he needs to go to the bathroom. We'd better put some newspaper down, too, just in case."

Christy carefully unpacked the box, admiring the cute bowls Aunt Nell had bought, with little bones painted on them, and the soft, red padded basket.

"Look! There's a collar and leash!" Christy exclaimed.

"Oh, yes," Dad nodded. "We'll have to get a tag with our phone number on it to put on the collar, just in case Lucky ever gets lost."

Dad held out a big bag. "Here's the food. Should I open it, Christy? Then you can give him some."

Christy carefully used the measuring cup to fill the bowl with food—Aunt Nell had explained about measuring out the right amount of puppy chow for Lucky's size. As she put the bowl down, Lucky immediately stopped sniffing his way along the kitchen cabinets and raced for the food bowl like some sort of trained sniffer dog. He gulped down the morsels in huge  mouthfuls, licking all the way around the bowl, just in case he'd missed some. Then he took a long drink of water.

"His tummy's almost touching the ground!" Christy pointed out. It was true. Lucky's little dachshund legs meant he wasn't that high off the ground anyway, and now his stomach looked like a small balloon underneath him. He gave a huge yawn, licked around his mouth again, and then looked for somewhere to collapse and sleep off his enormous snack. He stomped over to his basket, where Christy had put the special blanket that Aunt Nell had given them. She'd explained that it had been in the pen with Maisy and the puppies for the last few days, so that Lucky would have something that smelled familiar.

"Oh, Anna!" Mom sighed.

Lucky's new bed was already occupied. Anna was curled up in the soft basket, fast asleep. Lucky looked at her doubtfully, and then turned to look up at Christy, with his ears perked up just a little in a *Well, what am I supposed to do about this?* sort of way.

Mom gently lifted Anna out of the basket, but Lucky clearly wasn't sure about it now. He stood at Christy's feet, staring up at her pleadingly, and she knelt down next to him. Lucky gave a little sigh of relief and heaved himself onto her lap, circling around her knees a couple of times, and then slumping down in a heap—fast asleep.

Lucky settled into his new home very quickly. And he was growing up, too. He was still small—he was never going to be a big dog—but during the next couple of weeks, he stopped sleeping so much and became more and more adventurous—and a bit naughty. He loved playing in the yard with Christy and Anna, especially digging in the flowerbeds. Then he would trot happily back to the girls, covered in leaves and twigs, and shake himself all over them.

He was also terribly nosy. As soon as he was allowed out of the kitchen, after the first couple of days, he investigated the entire house. Every time Christy wasn't watching he would manage to find himself another secret hiding place, which he would get stuck in. Then he'd howl so she had to come and rescue him. Christy didn't understand how he actually managed to find half the spots, let alone climb into them. When he got trapped behind the washing machine, Dad had to pull it out from the wall for Lucky to escape.

For a dog with such short legs, he was a very good climber, although he was much better at climbing up than down. That never stopped him, though.

About a week after they'd gotten Lucky, Christy let him out into the yard on his own for the first time. Up until now she'd always gone with him, but he needed to go outside to do his business, and she was helping Mom cook.

Christy had just set the oven timer for the chocolate chip cookies they were baking when she realized that Lucky was still outside. She looked out of the kitchen window, but she couldn't see him.

"Maybe he's sitting by the door, waiting to come in," Mom suggested.

But he wasn't. Worried, Christy ran outside, hoping that Lucky hadn't found a gap under the fence. She and Dad had gone all the way around the yard, checking it for holes when they'd first brought him home, but what if they'd missed one?

She raced around the yard, calling anxiously. "Lucky! Lucky!"

Mom stood on the patio, carrying Anna, and peered into the flowerbeds.

Suddenly, Anna laughed and pointed,

and Christy heard a worried little whine somewhere up above her.

"Lucky! How did you get up there?"

He was standing in the doorway of Christy's treehouse, staring down uncertainly. The treehouse had been Christy's birthday present the year before, and it had steps built around the tree trunk. Obviously Lucky had managed to scramble up, but he wasn't so sure about getting down again.

"Oh, Lucky! You aren't supposed to go climbing!"

Dachshunds' long backs meant stairs weren't good for them—Christy was amazed that he had even managed to get up the steps. She reached for Lucky, and he wriggled into her arms gratefully so she could carry him down. Then he ran all around the yard twice, as though he liked the feel of solid ground under his paws.

Getting stuck in the treehouse didn't teach Lucky to be any more cautious, as Christy had hoped it might. He was still only a very little dog, but he seemed to think he was enormous, and he had no fear at all.

A few weeks after they had brought him home, once he had had all his vaccinations and been microchipped, Lucky was ready to go out for his first walk. Christy got out his beautiful blue leash. They were taking Lucky to the park—and she knew he would love it!

"Lucky, keep still!" She was trying to clip the leash on to his collar but Lucky kept wriggling. He'd never worn the leash before, but somehow he knew it meant something exciting.

"Let me check your collar, too…," Christy whispered. Aunt Nell had told her that it was important to fit his collar correctly—not so loose that it would slip off, but not so tight that it would rub. She was supposed to be able to put her finger between Lucky's neck and the collar. "I'll open it up one more hole, because it's a little tight on you. Lucky, stop jumping!" She giggled as he wriggled again and licked her nose.

Christy was a little worried that Lucky would be nervous as they walked to the park—especially with the noisy cars speeding past. But he bounced along happily, sniffing everything they passed. His claws clicked busily on the pavement as he scurried from side to side, occasionally darting behind Christy as he caught another interesting smell. Christy kept having to stop and unwind the leash from around her ankles.

"Are you all right, Christy? Do you want me to take him?" Dad asked.

Mom was walking with Anna,

who was just as much trouble as Lucky, and didn't have a leash, unfortunately.

"No, thank you." Christy shook her head firmly. Lucky was her special responsibility, and she had to be able to take care of him. Surely it couldn't be *that* difficult to go for a walk!

At last they reached the park. It wasn't very far away, but Lucky had probably covered three times the distance by going forward, backward, and sideways, and he was looking a little tired. But as soon as he saw the huge expanse of green grass, and the other dogs racing around, he brightened up immediately, his tail starting to whip from side to side. He sniffed busily at several clumps of grass, and then followed Christy along one of the paths.

"Should we see what he thinks of the ducks?" Dad suggested.

"Knowing Lucky, he'll think that they were put there for him to play with," Mom sighed. But they headed through the park toward the ducks, with Anna running ahead—the ducks were her favorite!

"Oh, watch out, Anna!" Mom called, seeing a man coming down the path with a big German shepherd. Anna loved dogs, and she wanted to pet all of them—even if they looked big and scary, like this one.

Lucky spotted the German shepherd at the same moment as Anna did, and he darted forward, dragging his leash out of Christy's hand.

"Lucky!" Christy squeaked in horror, watching him galloping away.

She looked down at her hand, as though she was still expecting the leash to be in it. Then she raced after him.

Lucky ran up to the huge German shepherd and barked loud, shrill barks at it. He could see Anna next to the bigger dog. She was his, even if she did keep sleeping in his basket. He wasn't going to let some big strange dog scare her. He danced around the huge dog—barking and yapping until he ran out of breath and had to sit down, panting.

The poor German shepherd hadn't even thought of hurting Anna, and was too well-trained to do anything to Lucky, either. She took a confused step backward, toward her owner. She was worried that she might be in trouble, and it was all very unfair.

But her owner patted her. "Good girl, Taffy. Sit. That's a good girl." The man then reached down and picked up Lucky in one hand—while Lucky wriggled and yapped and fought.

Christy came running up. Mom and Dad were chasing after them, too.

"Here you go." The man handed the wriggling puppy to Christy.

"I'm really sorry! It's his first walk—he doesn't really understand other dogs yet...," Christy stammered, hoping the German shepherd's owner wasn't going to shout at her.

"Sorry!" Dad gasped, as he picked up Anna. "I hope he didn't upset your dog."

Lucky was still yapping at the German shepherd, who was now sitting quietly and looking rather smug, as though she knew she was well-behaved and the little yappy dog wasn't.

"It's okay. Just be careful. Not all dogs are as calm as Taffy," her owner told Christy kindly, and he nodded at Dad.

"I won't let him run off again," Christy promised.

"I'm so sorry about that!" Dad said, holding Anna tightly, who was reaching out hopefully as the big dog paced past. "No, Anna, you can't pet her. We shouldn't have let you get so close."

"Let's go home before we get into any more trouble," Mom said, looking around anxiously at all the other dogs in the park.

As the German shepherd and her owner headed off down the path, Christy hugged Lucky tight. He was still staring suspiciously after the bigger dog, his little body tense with anxiety as he twisted in her arms.

"Oh, Lucky!" she whispered. "That dog could have eaten a puppy like you for breakfast!"

"And had room for a couple more," Dad added grimly.

Chapter Three

"It was so embarrassing," Christy said, blushing as she remembered the disastrous walk the day before. "And then on the way back home there was another big dog—a Labrador—and Lucky barked at him, too!"

Christy had hurried into school that morning to talk to Beth before they went into class. Beth had known they were taking Lucky for his first walk that weekend—Christy had been so excited about it on Friday.

Beth nodded. "I wonder if it's a small dog thing. My grandmother has a Westie named Buster, and he barks at *everything*. Grandma says it's because he knows he's little and he feels like he's got a lot to prove. Lucky might grow out of it," she suggested, a bit doubtfully.

Christy sighed. "Maybe. He's so sweet most of the time—you know he is. But I just couldn't get him to stop barking! Mom called Aunt Nell, and she says we need to take him to obedience classes. So Mom signed him up for some, but they don't start for a few weeks. I don't know what we're going to do until then!"

"I'm sure puppy training will help. He isn't really bad-tempered. Just yappy. He's a beautiful dog, Christy." Beth smiled, remembering. When she'd gone over to Christy's house last week, Lucky had curled up on her lap and fallen asleep. When it was time for Beth to go home, Christy had had to pick him up off her lap still asleep and all dangly, like a stuffed animal.

"Maybe he just needs to get used to other dogs," Christy said. "Or maybe you're right, and he will grow out of it. But I need to make sure I hold on to him really tightly until he does."

Beth frowned thoughtfully. "Couldn't you take him somewhere quieter for walks for now?" she suggested. "Somewhere with not as many dogs, I mean."

Christy nodded. "That's a good idea. I'll ask Mom and Dad if they can think of anywhere. It's fall break next week, so we should have more time for walks." She hugged Beth quickly as the bell rang. "Great idea!"

Christy's mom liked the idea of a quiet walk. She thought that it would be a fun way to start the fall break, after school on Friday afternoon.

"What about those woods we go past

on the way to your dance class? Maple Grove Park?" she suggested. "People do take their dogs there, but I doubt that many people would be out in the middle of a Friday afternoon."

"That would be great!" Christy agreed.

When they got out of school on Friday, she said good-bye to Beth— who was going to stay at her grandma's place for the week—and rushed to the car, flinging her bag into the back seat.

Lucky was sitting in his new wire travel crate, looking worried. He still wasn't sure about going in the car, and he wasn't really happy about being shut in the crate, but at least he had more space than in the old cardboard carrier.

The woods were only about a 15-minute drive away, and soon Christy was lifting Lucky out, letting him sniff busily at the grass. There were only a couple of other cars there—it looked like the woods would be empty.

It was a beautiful autumn day, really warm for October, and Lucky had a wonderful time racing along with Christy, and flinging himself into piles of dry leaves. They flew everywhere as he rolled and jumped and snapped at them, growling as though he were very fierce. His legs were so short that every so often he disappeared right into a drift of leaves, and then he would come up spluttering and do it all over again.

Christy was laughing so much her tummy hurt. The way Lucky's ears flapped when he jumped made him look like he were trying to take off!

"Oooh, river!" Anna called excitedly, as they came to a little stream running along between deep, sloping banks.

There was an old rickety-looking wooden bridge, and they stood on it throwing sticks in and watching them float past underneath the bridge. Lucky watched them in bewilderment, unsure why anyone would waste good sticks by dropping them in the water. He whined and tugged on the leash, wanting to go and explore some more, and at last they went over the bridge and deeper into the woods.

Christy and Lucky were chasing Anna through the leaves when suddenly Lucky stopped, staring off down the little path they were following. He'd heard something, Christy could tell. He looked as though he were listening with every hair of his body. Then she heard it, too—barking, but much further into the woods. They weren't going to have the place to themselves after all.

"Oh, is it another dog?" Mom said with a sigh. "Hold on to him tightly, Christy. Or I can take him, if you want."

"It's okay, Mom." Christy wound the leash around her hand as Lucky let off a series of earsplitting barks. He jumped around at the end of his leash, wanting to chase after the other dog, but Christy wouldn't let go.

Anna stared at Lucky, wide-eyed. She didn't like it when Lucky barked loudly. She backed away, meaning to grab a hold of Mom's hand, but she wasn't looking where she was going. She tripped over a tree root and fell, scraping the side of her face against the rocky ground.

"Oh, Anna!" Mom came running to scoop her up as she started to howl.

Lucky was so surprised by the noise

Anna was making that he stopped barking. He didn't like loud noises, either—unless he was the one making them. He whimpered and pulled at his leash, trying to get away.

"Christy, can you get the wipes out of my bag?" Mom asked, examining the scrape down the side of Anna's face.

Christy nodded. But Lucky was pulling and tugging at the leash, and she couldn't unzip the bag and hold him at the same time. She looped Lucky's leash over a nearby branch so she could open the bag. "Here they are."

Lucky wriggled anxiously. He didn't like to see Anna upset, and he certainly didn't like the wailing. But once Mom found a couple of pieces of candy in her bag, Anna seemed to cheer up miraculously, and let her wipe the scrape clean. After that, Lucky stopped worrying about Anna and started to investigate the branch that Christy had fastened him to.

He didn't like it. He couldn't move more than half a foot either way without the leash pulling on his collar and hurting his neck. He couldn't go and sniff at that clump of leaves, which smelled as though a couple of other dogs had been there before. He *had* to check that out. And there was a really good, big stick just out of reach that he would love to chew. It wasn't fair! He shook himself impatiently, making the tags on his collar jingle.

"It's all right, Lucky, hang on a minute...," Christy said. But she didn't even look at him—she was still helping Mom with Anna.

Lucky shook himself again, and his leash slipped off the end of the branch and thudded to the ground beside him. He stared at it in surprise. He hadn't meant for that to happen.

If Anna hadn't started to howl again,

because Mom had accidentally wiped her face too hard, Christy would have noticed what had happened and grabbed him. But she was giving Anna a hug to cheer her up.

Lucky eyed them thoughtfully. They were busy. But there was no point in coming out for a walk, and then just sitting on the path the whole time. He padded away, sniffing happily at the leaves. He expected that Christy would come and catch him up in a minute anyway. Another dog had definitely been past—maybe the one he'd heard barking earlier. He would go and find it. He scampered along the path, nose down, following the scent, and leaving Christy and Anna and Mom far behind.

"Is she going to be okay?" Christy

asked Mom worriedly. It looked like a nasty cut, and it was still bleeding, even after Mom had wiped it a couple of times.

"She'll be fine," Mom said. "We need to go home and wash the scrape, though."

"It hurts!" Anna wailed. "An' my fleece! My best fleece!" It was her pink one with the hearts on it, and it was covered with mud all down the side.

"Mom can wash it. It'll be dry by tomorrow, won't it, Mom?" Christy hugged her little sister gently. "Lucky didn't mean to scare you by barking like that. He thought he heard another dog. Didn't you, Lucky?"

Christy turned around to look at him. But Lucky was gone.

Chapter Four

The woods were full of birds calling, and squirrels racing up and down the branches. Lucky was so little and so light-footed that on his own, without Mom and the girls, he hardly made any noise at all—only the quiet shushing of his leash, trailing behind him through the leaves. So he saw more of the wildlife than he had before. A robin fluttered from tree to tree—almost as if it were leading him down the path—and Lucky followed, fascinated.

The woods were old, and some of the trees were very large, with odd twisted roots that made little bridges and holes along the path. It was natural for such a small dog to try to wriggle through these rather than going around them, but unfortunately Lucky forgot about his leash. He was hurrying after the robin when he was pulled back with a sudden, horrible jolt. He yelped and turned around, thinking that Christy had caught up with him and grabbed the end of his leash. He looked up angrily. Why hadn't she called him, instead of grabbing him like that? But Christy wasn't there.

Instead, his leash was caught on a root that was sticking out of the ground—really stuck, as he found out when he tried to pull it away like he had earlier. Lucky wriggled, and whined, and whimpered, and pulled, but it was no good. The leash wasn't budging this time.

Lucky sat down, panting wearily. This was just the same as before—he was stuck, when he wanted to explore. He tried pulling again, this time the other way, squirming backward to pull off his collar instead of trying to free the leash.

As usual, Christy had checked Lucky's collar before they set out to make sure there was enough space so it didn't rub him and hurt. But that also meant that if Lucky didn't mind squashing his ears and wriggling very hard, it wasn't actually that difficult to get the collar off.

He burst out of it like a cork from a bottle, rolling over backward and landing in a pile of leaves. He picked himself up and sniffed curiously at his collar and leash. He didn't want to leave them. But he was sure Christy would come along soon, and she could unhook the silly leash for him. He'd let her put it back on him if she'd come and run with him, instead of standing around and spoiling a good walk.

He trotted off through the undergrowth. He'd lost sight of the robin, but now there was an interesting furry, gray creature that was scampering through the branches above him. He wasn't sure what it was, but it bounced and sprang very temptingly, and he was hoping it might come a little lower. He barked at it, but that made it go faster and climb higher, and he had to run to keep up.

"Lucky! Lucky!" came a far-off cry. That was Christy calling him. He stopped for a second, but the squirrel stopped, too, looking down at him so teasingly that he couldn't bear to let it go. He'd try to find Christy in a minute, once he'd caught the squirrel. He set off on a gallop again, and the squirrel leaped through the trees ahead of him.

He was chasing it so desperately that he almost ran into a lady standing in the middle of a clump of bushes, holding a pair of binoculars.

"Shhh!" the lady whispered angrily.

Lucky stopped short, staring at her in surprise. She'd been so quiet that he simply hadn't noticed she was there.

There was a beating of wings and a pair of birds fluttered away, squawking in fright. Lucky watched them go and barked again excitedly.

The lady sighed. "You've scared them away, you silly dog." Then she seemed to realize for the first time that he was all alone. "Where's your owner, hmm?" She looked around, expecting someone to come chasing after him, but the woods were silent. "You don't have a collar! Who do you belong to? They shouldn't be letting you race around here on your own; there's a road close by. Come here.... Here, dog...."

She stretched out a hand to him, but Lucky had heard the irritated tone in her voice after he scared the birds, and now he didn't trust her. He backed away nervously, and as she took a step forward to grab him, he raced off.

He hurried back through the bushes to the path, suddenly wishing that he were with Christy. He'd find her, and then maybe they'd be able to catch the strange furry, gray animal in the trees together. Lucky scurried down the path, expecting at any moment to come to the big trees where he'd lost his leash, and then, a little further, to find Mom and Anna and, most importantly, Christy.

But as he went further and further along, Lucky realized that this might not be the path he wanted. He looked around, and suddenly the trees all seemed so much larger and darker, and different. He had no idea where he was, or where Christy was. He was lost.

"But we can't just leave him!" Christy stared at her mom in horror.

"Christy, we have to go. I'm sorry. We've been searching for a long time." Mom was holding Anna in her arms, who was crying miserably, the scrape on her face still bleeding a little. "I need to get Anna home and clean up her face. It's filthy, and it's been like this for almost an hour."

"If we go home now, we might never find Lucky! Just five more minutes, please, Mom." Christy looked around, desperately hoping Lucky might spring out of the bushes suddenly, and everything would be all right again. But they had searched everywhere, calling and calling. Lucky seemed to have totally disappeared.

"I've called your dad, and he's going to leave work early so you can both come right back and look. I'm really sorry, sweetheart, but we have to get home." Mom set off down the path, carrying Anna.

Christy stood in the middle of the path, looking uncertainly one way and then the other. She couldn't bear the thought of leaving Lucky. Maybe he'd been frightened by something and was hiding. He might come out in just a minute, if they were quiet.

"Christy, please!" Mom called, heading for the bridge over the stream.

Christy trailed after her, trying not to cry. But by the time they reached the car, the tears were streaming down her face.

Lucky padded down another path, sniffing hopefully. He was sure he could smell Christy, but the scent was all over the place. It was very confusing. It didn't help that he was hungry. He wanted to be back at home with Christy, eating his dinner.

Just then, he heard the rushing sound of the stream, and he trotted forward, peering down the steep bank at the water. They had come over the stream, and that had been before Anna had fallen over, he remembered.

He sat down at the top of the bank. Should he cross over again or not? He whimpered miserably, wishing he had run back to Christy when she called him. No. He wouldn't cross over it again. Christy would wait for him where he'd left her, he was sure. By those big trees, where Anna had fallen down. He only had to find them. He turned away from the stream and nosed along, trying to find the path. But so many dogs had walked through the woods that he was distracted and kept losing Christy's scent.

It was starting to get dark, and the woods were gloomy, and full of strange noises, rustlings, and odd bird calls. For the first time, Lucky began to wonder what else might be in the woods, besides that gray creature he'd chased. He wondered if there was anything bigger.

The late afternoon shadows meant that Lucky didn't even notice when he padded over the stream further along its course, where it ran under a fence in a huge metal pipe. Lucky was small enough not to pay much attention to the fence—he simply went under it— and he didn't see the pipe buried in the bank. So he was surprised to find himself almost back at the road.

He came around a corner of the path and pulled up quickly, staring at the wider road at the edge of the path that led into the woods. He knew this place! He was sure of it, even though he hadn't crossed the stream again. This was just a little further from where they had left their car. But the space they had parked in was empty.

They had left without him!

Chapter Five

Lucky sat down on the path miserably. He'd been just about to find Christy, he was sure of it. But it looked like she'd left without him. He couldn't understand why she would go away and leave him. Didn't she want him back? Was she angry because he'd frightened Anna?

He whimpered, staring across the road at the space where the car should have been. Then he whirled around, his tail tucked in, and a tiny growl beginning in his throat.

Behind him was a tall man who'd come jogging down the path, his big white sneakers shining, even in the gathering dusk.

"Hey, it's all right. I almost stepped on you, didn't I, you poor little thing. I'm sorry—I didn't see you there. I was just running, and not really looking." The man crouched down, panting, and stared at Lucky, smiling. "You might just be the smallest dog I've ever seen."

Lucky glared back at him suspiciously, remembering the lady who had scolded him before.

The man held out a gentle hand, and Lucky sniffed at it. The man smelled like another dog, which wasn't good, but aside from that, Lucky felt as though he could trust him. And he didn't know what else to do.

"Who do you belong to? You're not a stray; you're very well taken care of. Beautiful shiny coat, and you're not skinny, even if you are a tiny thing. Where's your collar? I bet you've slipped out of your leash, haven't you? Someone's going to be really worried about you."

Lucky backed away slightly as the man's hand went to his pocket, but all he did was pull out something in a crinkly wrapper and open it. He broke off a piece and held it out to Lucky.

"It's not really the best thing to give a dog, but a little bit won't do you any harm. You try it, pup. It's good. I like them, especially when I've been out for a run. It's an energy bar."

The thing smelled sweet and sugary, and it was making Lucky hungrier than ever. He darted forward and snapped it out of the man's hand, swallowing it in one gulp.

"Nice, isn't it? Want some more? I wonder who you belong to. You must have come here on a walk with your owners, because there are no houses close by, and you're too little to have come far on your own." The man looked around thoughtfully. "So where are they, hmm? I don't want to leave you galloping through the woods on your own, and it's starting to get dark."

He stood up again and looked around. "Hello! Anyone lost a dog?"

The shout echoed through the trees, but no one answered. The only sound now was a light pattering, as it began to rain.

"We're going to get soaked." He looked down at Lucky, who was shivering and pressing himself back against the bushes. "Sorry, pup. Did I scare you, shouting like that?"

He broke off another piece of the energy bar, and this time Lucky nibbled it out of his hand, and let the man pet his head and ears. "Yes, you're a beautiful little boy, aren't you?" He sighed. "What are we going to do with you? There are no cars left, and I can't hear anyone else around. I can't just leave you here on your own. You don't look to me like you've got any road sense at all...."

He stretched out his hand again, and this time Lucky sniffed it eagerly, hoping for more food. But the man picked him up instead, very gently, but firmly enough that Lucky didn't feel as though he was going to be dropped. He snuggled against the man's warm hoodie, feeling a tiny bit better. Of course, the man wasn't the same as Christy, but he was warm, and friendly, and the sugary stuff was very nice.

"Come on, then. You'd better come home with me, while I call the dog shelter." The man tucked Lucky in the crook of his arm and set off down the road.

Lucky stared back at the trees, and the greenish gloomy darkness that was settling between them. He didn't like it here. But what if Christy came back for him and he'd disappeared? He wriggled in the man's arms, and howled. He had to stay and wait for Christy! Surely she was going to come back! And now he wouldn't be there for her!

"Shhh, shhh, I know. But I can't leave you here, pup. Don't worry. We'll find your owners, I promise." The man frowned. "Well, I hope so, anyway…."

On her way back to the woods with Dad, Christy peered anxiously out of the car window. She'd read so many stories about dogs finding their way home that she half-expected to see Lucky trotting down the road toward them.

"Dad!" She pointed to the grassy area. "We parked here, and went up that path." She looked at her watch. It had been an hour since they'd left. She'd had to wait for Dad to get home, and then they'd driven all the way back. Lucky had been missing for two whole hours now.

Her dad parked the car. "Come on, then." He got out, and peered into the darkening woods. "Don't worry, Christy. He's probably just hiding from the rain."

Christy shivered. Somehow the woods looked much less welcoming than they had after school, when the autumn sun had been bright and friendly. But she straightened her shoulders, and marched determinedly up the path, calling for Lucky. He had to be here somewhere.

"Can you remember where Anna fell?" Dad asked, rushing after her. "He might have had the sense to go back to where you left him."

"I think so. It wasn't far from here, just on the other side of the stream." Christy hurried on, crossing over the bridge, and looking anxiously from side to side, calling until her throat started to hurt.

"I can't understand why he isn't coming," she told her dad, stopping at the top of a little slope, and staring around them hopelessly. "I know he's naughty, but he usually comes if I call him in the yard. He knows I'll give him treats and cuddle him. Why doesn't he want to come back to us now?" She leaned against her dad, trying hard not to cry. If she started, she knew it would be hard to stop.

"Christy, don't worry. This place must be full of amazing smells for a dog." Dad hugged her. "He's bound to be off chasing a squirrel or something. And remember what he was like when we met that German shepherd in the park? He might have chased after another dog."

"We did hear another dog barking." Christy nodded. "But it sounded like it was a long way away. Dad, he could be *anywhere,*" she added. "What if he ran on to the road?" she whispered.

Her dad sighed, and hugged her tighter. "I don't think he'd do that, Christy. He's never tried it before, has he?"

"He's only been on a couple of walks," Christy pointed out miserably. "And if he saw another dog he might."

Her dad shook his head. "There's no reason to think he went on to the road. He's probably sitting under a tree waiting for you. He'll be angry that you left him, knowing Lucky!" Dad was trying to be cheerful, Christy knew, but it wasn't really working.

She kept walking and calling, but still no Lucky, or even an answering bark.

"Hey, what's that?" her dad asked, pointing at a flash of blue among a mass of twisted roots.

"His leash! That's Lucky's leash!" Christy's heart jumped wildly as she scrambled for it, hoping that she might find Lucky curled up fast asleep at the other end. He did sleep very deeply sometimes; he might not have heard them calling.

But all she found on the end of the leash was Lucky's collar.

"Oh, Lucky…," she whispered.

"He must have slipped it off," Dad said grimly. "Well, at least we know he was here. Come on, let's keep looking. We've got about another half-hour before it's completely dark."

Christy swallowed as she looked around at the massive, hulking trees. There were holes and hiding places all over the woods, and it was getting darker by the minute. She was scared, and she was with Dad.

And if she was scared, Christy couldn't help thinking as they hurried deeper into the trees, how frightened must Lucky be, all alone!

Chapter Six

"I wish I knew what your name was," the man said to Lucky, as he carried him down the road and back toward town. "I suppose I'm going to have to keep calling you pup. I'm Jake, by the way," he added, smiling down at Lucky, who was curled into his elbow, watching everything they passed with anxious eyes. "And we're going back to my place, just for a little while, and then we'll take you to the shelter. Then hopefully your owners will come and find you...."

Lucky glanced up at Jake's face, his ears flattening a little. There was a worried tone to the man's voice again, and he didn't like it.

"Yes, I know. No one would leave you behind on purpose, surely...." He sighed. "Anyway, we're almost home. You're going to meet Mickey." He laughed. "Mickey's going to get a shock when he sees you. I only went out for a quick jog."

He searched in the pockets of his sweatpants for the keys as they came up to a little white house. Lucky leaned forward, listening intently. He could hear the clicking of claws on a hard floor, and a curious snuffling. There was another dog in there! It had to be the one that the man smelled like. He shifted a little nervously in Jake's arms. Usually he barked and barked at other dogs, but then he'd been with Christy. Lucky wanted everyone to know that she was his, and he was taking care of Anna and her.

As the door swung open, a golden-brown head peered slowly around it and stared suspiciously up at Lucky.

"Hey, boy. I've brought a visitor. Don't worry. I don't think he's staying that long." Jake tucked Lucky tightly under his arm, and crouched down to give some attention to his old golden retriever, muttering a stream of reassuring words.

"It's lucky you're such a good boy, Mickey. You're not jealous. The pup's lost, poor little thing. We're going to help him get back home, that's all."

Mickey eyed Lucky thoughtfully, as the dachshund puppy stared back. Then he wagged his long, feathery tail a couple of times, very slowly, and turned around, pacing back toward the kitchen and his cushion.

"You're going to have to be gentle with Mickey," Jake told Lucky. "He's an old gentleman. Twelve years old, and he's a bit lame now. Don't go teasing him!" He put Lucky down, watching carefully to see how he and Mickey were going to get along. Jake knew Mickey was really gentle, but he wasn't used to having other dogs in his house.

Lucky looked around nervously, and then sidled after Jake as he headed into the kitchen, too.

"I know there's a flier from Oakleaf Rescue Shelter here somewhere. I was going to send them some money...," Jake muttered, searching through a pile of papers. "And now I'm sending them a wiener dog instead!" He pulled out a piece of paper covered in photos of dogs. "Ah, good. You two all right?" He looked down at Mickey, now curled up in his basket. Lucky was sniffing thoroughly around the kitchen cupboards, and keeping his distance from the bigger dog. "Okay. Let's call them." He tapped in the number, and then sighed. "I should have known. It's six o'clock already. No one's answering the phone." He put the phone back in its cradle slowly, and stared at Lucky. "Now what do we do with you, pup? We'd better feed you, I suppose. That energy bar won't keep you going for long."

He took a small bowl out of the cupboard and put it down a little way from Mickey's big dog bowl, then poured food into both of them from a huge bag.

Lucky flung himself at it as though he were starving and gulped it down.

"Hopefully senior dog food won't do you any harm this once," Jake said, watching with a smile as Lucky gobbled the dry food. "Let's get you some water, too."

Lucky finished his food and took a long drink of water. Then he watched Mickey, who was still slowly eating his bowlful of food. He edged a little closer, and Mickey turned around and gave him a very meaningful stare. *Don't come near my dinner.*

Lucky wriggled backward on his bottom, and then scuttled under the kitchen table until Mickey had finished and paced back to his bed for an after-dinner snooze.

"You need to be careful, pup," Jake told him, petting his head. "Mickey's a lot bigger than you, and this is his house."

But Lucky was a naturally confident little dog, and he didn't really understand how small he was, either. He was starting to feel a bit more at home now, and he pranced up to Mickey, eyeing the bigger dog with his head to one side.

Mickey stared back, his muzzle resting on the edge of his cushion. He was a beautiful golden color, but his coat was turning silvery now, all around his mouth and eyes. He yawned, showing his very large teeth, and Lucky took a step back again, looking a bit more respectful.

Even the teeth didn't stop him for long, though. Lucky wasn't used to being ignored, and he didn't like it. He padded right up to Mickey and yapped sharply at him.

Mickey laid his ears back. The strange little dog was barking at him now, when he was trying to sleep.

Jake took a few steps closer. He trusted Mickey, but he wasn't taking any chances.

Lucky wagged his tail excitedly and barked again, even louder, wanting to get a reaction out of the bigger dog.

Mickey looked over at Jake, his eyes wide, as if he were saying, *Rescue me from this thing!* But Jake only watched, smiling a little.

Lucky crept closer, head down with his front paws flat against the kitchen floor, yapping and whining, his tail wagging. He was starting to enjoy this now. Maybe the big dog was scared of him!

Mickey huffed out a deep, irritable breath, and stood up, towering over the curious puppy. He put out a massive golden paw, and stood on one of Lucky's too-long dachshund ears.

Lucky wriggled and whined, but Mickey had him pinned. It was a clear message. *This is my house. You do as you're told.*

The puppy rolled over—as far as he could with Mickey holding his ear down—waving his paws in the air to show he gave in, and at last Mickey removed his paw. Lucky stayed on his back, showing off his tummy apologetically, until Mickey sat down in his bed.

Finally, Lucky turned over and wriggled forward, creeping closer to the cushion as Mickey watched him. At the edge of the cushion, the puppy looked up hopefully, and the old dog nuzzled him. With a pleased little squeak, Lucky scurried onto the cushion, and sat down next to Mickey. He did keep glancing up at the big dog, though, to make sure he wasn't about to get the ear treatment again.

Jake laughed. "Taught him his place, have you, Mickey? Can he share your bed for tonight, then?"

Mickey sighed, and slumped down on the cushion, squishing Lucky up against the edge. But the puppy didn't seem to mind. He closed his eyes and snuggled himself up to Mickey's broad back, so he was half-lying on top of the bigger dog—and then the two of them went to sleep.

"Where's Lucky?" Anna asked, as Christy pushed open the kitchen door, the leash dangling from her hand.

Her little sister was sitting at the table with their mom, eating a eating a snack. There was a big white gauze square over her scratched face, but she looked much more cheerful.

Christy gulped, and then turned around and raced upstairs to her bedroom. She couldn't face explaining to Anna. And then she was going to have to tell Aunt Nell that they'd lost her precious puppy, too!

She sat down on her floor, leaning against the warm radiator and sniffing. Lucky liked to snuggle up here, too. He wasn't allowed to sleep in her room, but she carried him up to play sometimes.

Her bedroom door creaked open slowly, and Anna peered around it. "Are you angry?" she whispered.

Christy shook her head. She hadn't thought to be angry with Anna—her little sister hadn't meant to fall over.

"Did Lucky run away cuz I fell over?" Anna said sadly.

Christy put out her arms for Anna to come and hug her. "It wasn't your fault. I should have taken care of him better."

"Oh, Christy! You were helping me take care of Anna." She hadn't seen her mom come in, too. "It was just an unfortunate accident. I'm sure we'll find Lucky. Dad can take you back to the woods really early in the morning."

Christy nodded, but tears were sliding down her cheeks. "He'll be scared out there, Mom. It's so dark—there are streetlights here, but there aren't any out there in the woods! And he'll be cold and hungry." She hugged Anna tighter, and her sister snuggled against her.

"We'll find him tomorrow, Christy, I promise," Mom said.

Christy nodded. But how could Mom promise that when no one knew where Lucky was?

"Hey, pup!"

Lucky yawned and opened his eyes. Why was Christy waking him up, in the dark?

Then he sat up quickly, looking around in panic. That wasn't Christy!

"Shhh, don't worry. I just thought you might need a quick trip out to the yard before I go to bed. I'm not sure if you're house-trained yet." Jake opened the back door, and the security light came on, sending an orange light into the kitchen, and all of a sudden, Lucky remembered where he was.

Or actually, where he *wasn't*. He wasn't at home in his comfy red basket with Christy asleep upstairs. He was lost.

He whimpered, staring out at the strange, dark yard.

"I know. We'll find your owners tomorrow, hopefully. We'll call the shelter again in the morning." Jake picked him up, and carried him out into the yard. "Go on, then you can go back to sleep."

Lucky wandered out onto the lawn, sniffing the night smell of wet grass. Everything was different, and wrong! Where was Christy? Why hadn't he just stayed and waited for her? Then he would be home by now.

He sat down, raised his head to the sky, and howled.

Chapter Seven

"What if someone's found him and doesn't know who he belongs to?" Christy said worriedly, looking back at Dad as they hurried into the woods early the next morning. It was chilly, and leaves were whirling in the cold wind.

"He's microchipped, too, remember," Dad pointed out. "If someone takes him to a vet or the dog shelter, they'll be able to scan his microchip, and then they'll call us."

"So why haven't they?" Christy wailed. "Maybe he got stuck down in a badger hole! Aunt Nell said that a long time ago, dachshunds were bred to chase badgers down their holes. Are there badgers in Maple Grove Park, Dad?"

"Probably," Dad admitted. "But I don't think Lucky would chase one...."

"He would!" Christy told him sadly. "He tried to show that German shepherd who was boss, didn't he?"

"Excuse me...," someone behind them called breathlessly.

Christy wheeled around in surprise. She'd been so busy imagining Lucky stuck down a badger's hole that she hadn't seen the lady coming up the path behind them. She hadn't expected anyone else to be here at seven thirty in the morning.

"Have you lost a dog? I'm sorry, I heard you calling…."

"Yes!" Dad replied, and Christy raced up to the lady.

"Have you seen my puppy?" she gasped. "Do you know where he is?"

"A little brown-and-black dachshund? I saw him yesterday—I come here to do birdwatching, you see. I did try to catch him, as I thought he might be lost, but he ran off again."

"That's Lucky," Christy whispered. "Did you see which way he went?" she added, rather hopelessly.

"No, but...," the lady paused thoughtfully. "There was a man jogging, and I saw him again as I went back home. He had a little dog with him, and it might have been the same one...."

"Someone took Lucky!" Christy gasped. "He stole him! He must have, or why didn't he call us?"

Dad hugged her. "Don't panic. Lucky slipped out of his collar, remember? Maybe the man took him to the police station. Or the dog shelter in town! That's more likely. We'll go home and call them. Thanks so much," he told the lady. "You've been really helpful."

"I hope you find him," the lady smiled. "He's a sweet little thing."

Christy nodded. She was right—Lucky was so little. Much too little to be out on his own. *He's at the shelter,* she told herself firmly. *He has to be....*

Dad put down the phone, making a face. "Answering machine. But the recorded message says Oakleaf Rescue Shelter opens at nine...."

He checked his watch. Christy had been up at six wanting to go back to Maple Grove Park, and it was still only eight thirty. "It'll take us about 20 minutes to get there," he said thoughtfully.

"Let's go!" Christy grabbed his hand and started pulling him toward the front door.

They sped off in the car, Christy waving to Mom and Anna, who were watching from the door. Anna was really missing Lucky, too. She'd been up almost as early as Christy had, and when Christy and Dad got back from the woods, Christy had found her little sister sitting in Lucky's basket, looking confused and sad.

As they drove through town to the shelter, Christy leaned forward, her fists clenched so tightly her arms ached.

"Relax, Christy," said Dad. "You're not making us go any faster. The shelter doesn't open for another 15 minutes, anyway, and we're almost there."

Christy was out of the car the moment they stopped in the parking lot, and she was off, running toward the doors to the shelter. But it was still locked, and she rattled it uselessly.

"It's only five of nine," Dad called, following her across the parking lot.

Christy paced up and down as they waited outside, checking her watch every 10 seconds or so, certain each time that it must be nine o'clock by now.

At last, they saw a figure coming toward the glass doors, and a young woman smiled at them as she put the key in the lock.

Christy hung on to Dad's arm, as the woman swung the door open. "Good morning!" she said cheerfully. "Have you come to adopt a dog?"

Dad shook his head. "I'm afraid not. We're really hoping that our puppy is here. We lost him yesterday afternoon."

"Oh, I see." The young woman looked doubtful. "I haven't heard about a puppy being brought in." She saw Christy's face fall, and added quickly, "But I wasn't here yesterday, so don't take my word for it. I'll have to check with one of the others. Come on in, anyway."

She led them into the reception area. Christy could hear the noise of barking from down the hallway that led into the main shelter area. She strained her ears, trying to hear Lucky's sharp, dachshund bark. But it was too hard to pick it out. There was a clang of metal, too, which she guessed was the food bowls being put out.

"There's nothing on the computer about a new puppy...." The woman was frowning as she tapped on the keyboard. "Let me go and ask Lucy. She's the manager, and she was in yesterday."

Christy swallowed. It felt like there was a huge lump stuck in her throat, and she was fighting back tears. "Dad, where can he be, if he's not here?" she whispered, choking on her words.

"Don't get ahead of yourself," Dad replied, hugging her. "He might be here." But he didn't sound all that hopeful.

A dark-haired woman came into the

reception area. "Hi, I'm Lucy Barnes. Andrea says you're looking for a lost puppy? I'm really sorry, but we didn't have any dogs brought in yesterday."

"None at all?" Dad asked worriedly.

"Where can he be, then?" Christy asked, giving up the fight with the tears, and feeling them trickle down her cheeks.

"It may take a couple of days for him to get to us," Lucy explained gently. "Don't give up. Someone may have found him, and they could be holding on to him to see if they can find the owner themselves."

"That man might have stolen him," Christy sobbed. "The lady said she saw a man carrying a dog."

"Let me write down your phone number, and some details about your puppy," Lucy suggested. "Then if someone brings him in to us, we'll get right back to you."

"Thanks. He's a dachshund puppy, 15 weeks old, and he's brown and black," Dad explained, and Lucy typed the details into the computer.

"His name is Lucky," Christy gulped.

"And he went missing yesterday?"

"Yes, from Maple Grove Park. He's microchipped—that should help, shouldn't it?" Dad asked hopefully.

Lucy smiled. "That's great. If he's brought in to the police, or to a vet, they'll call you right away."

"Okay. Well, thanks, Lucy. Come on, Christy." Dad led her out to the parking lot. "I'm sorry, sweetie. Look, we'll stop by the police station on the way back. Maybe he got taken there. And if not, we'll pick up some rolls of tape on the way home, then we can make some posters and put them up on all the lampposts."

Christy nodded, but tears started welling up in her eyes again. If they put up LOST posters, it meant they really had no idea where Lucky was at all.

Chapter Eight

Christy trailed across the parking lot, tears still trickling down her cheeks even though she kept wiping them away. Dad had his arm around her, but it wasn't making her feel any better.

Dad was just unlocking the car when Christy heard someone calling behind them, and running footsteps.

"Wait a minute!" Lucy, the center

manager, was chasing them across the parking lot, looking excited. She spoke into the phone in her hand, "Yes, I've caught them. A brown-and-black dachshund? That's wonderful!"

Christy turned around to look at Lucy, her eyes wide with sudden hope. "Someone's found him!" she whispered.

Lucy nodded at her, smiling hugely as she listened to whoever it was on the other end of the phone.

Christy felt like grabbing the phone. She wanted to know where Lucky was right now!

Finally Lucy ended the call, and grinned at Christy and Dad. "36 Elm Lane. A very nice-sounding man named Jake Harper went jogging in Maple Grove Park last night, and found a little brown-and-black dachshund puppy with no collar or leash. He called us, but we were closed, so he tried again just now to ask if it was okay to bring the puppy in." Her grin got even bigger. "I told him we'd save him the trouble and send you there instead! I hope you don't mind...."

"Thank you!" Christy flung her arms around Lucy and hugged her tightly. "Oh, that's the best news!" She let go and looked up at Lucy worriedly. "It has to be Lucky, hasn't it?" she asked. "There couldn't be another dachshund in the woods...."

"Jake was sure it was your puppy. The age sounded about right, and dachshunds aren't that common. Now go and get him!"

Dad smiled at Lucy. "Elm Lane, right? Thanks for all your help. Come on, Christy!"

"'Bye!" Christy jumped into the car, fighting with her seat belt. She was suddenly so nervous that her fingers seemed to have stopped working. It had to be Lucky, it just had to. She couldn't bear to be disappointed again.

Lucky was lying in the middle of the cushion, with his head on his paws, watching as Mickey ate his breakfast.

It was dog food from a tin this time—different than the food Lucky had at home. He liked the smell, but somehow he wasn't very hungry, even though there was also a big helping for him.

"You're quiet this morning." Jake crouched down by the basket. "I hope you're not sick. Especially since I think I've found your owner. A young lady's very worried about you, apparently. Maybe you're just missing her, mmm?" He stood up. "Well, it won't hurt you to miss one breakfast, I suppose, if you don't feel like it. Do you want to go outside? Quick sniff around the yard? No?" He patted Lucky's smooth head. "Not long now, pup. Cheer up."

Lucky had lifted his head to look at Jake while he was talking, but now that the big man was walking away, he let it flop back down. He didn't want food, and he didn't want to go out in the yard. He wanted Christy.

He wanted Christy pouring out his dog food, and watching him lovingly while he wolfed it down. He wanted to race up and down the yard with her and Anna. He liked Jake, and Mickey was good to share a bed with for one night. But he didn't want to stay here.

He'd never really known another dog before. Especially not one that stood on his ears! This was Mickey's house, and Jake was Mickey's special person. Mickey had made that very clear, and Lucky didn't mind. He just wanted to be back home with Christy.

Elm Lane wasn't far from the shelter, and Christy and her dad pulled up outside number 36 about 10 minutes later.

They could hear barking from inside, even before they rang the bell, and Christy looked up at Dad with shining eyes. It was a squeaky sort of bark. A bossy little dog's bark....

"It's him, isn't it?" Christy whispered,

and Dad nodded, beaming.

On the other side of the door, Lucky scratched and yelped, clawing at the wood panels. He could hear Christy! She'd come to find him!

As the door opened, a small brown-and-black ball of fur hurled itself at Christy, barking and yapping.

She picked him up, laughing and crying at the same time. "Lucky! Where did you go? We looked everywhere for you! Oh, I missed you!"

Lucky licked her face lovingly, then went back to jumping and wriggling, and wagging his tail so hard his whole back end wagged, too. He leaned dangerously far out of Christy's arms to lick Dad, too, and even licked Jake.

Jake laughed. "Yes, you're happy now, aren't you, pup?"

"Thank you for finding him," Christy said shyly, so quietly that Jake could hardly hear her over the loud barking.

"That's all right. He didn't have a collar. I guess he must have lost it."

"He was wearing one." Christy nodded. "My little sister, Anna, fell over a tree root, and I was helping Mom cheer her up. I hooked Lucky's leash over a branch, and by the time we'd calmed Anna down, he was just gone!" Her voice squeaked with fright as she remembered it. "I bet you went off chasing squirrels, didn't you?" she asked Lucky. "The woods were full of them."

Then her eyes widened, as Mickey lumbered into the hallway to see what was going on. "Oh! You've got a dog, too." She looked worriedly up at Dad, and then at Jake. "I'm really sorry if Lucky fought with him...."

Jake laughed. "Actually, he tried being a bit bossy, but Mickey stood on him. After that he was very good!"

"Stood on him?" Christy gasped, looking at Mickey. He was huge.

He looked like he could squash Lucky.

"Just on one ear, just for a moment. His way of showing Lucky who was in charge, I think. Has he been difficult with other dogs before, then?"

Christy shuddered. "He barks at them. It's like he thinks he's as big as they are." She looked down at Lucky, who'd wriggled out of her arms and was dancing around Mickey's legs, nuzzling him playfully. "But he's being so nice to your dog now!"

Jake grinned. "Maybe he just needed a lesson on who's in charge of the pack. Have you tried puppy parties?"

Dad shook his head. "I haven't even heard of them. Is it like training? We're registered for a class that starts in a couple of weeks."

"Oh, well, the people running your training might do puppy parties, too—you should ask. It's like a safe place for young dogs to get to know each other. It teaches them how to get along, and figure out who's in charge. But you're there to step in if there are any problems."

"You know a lot about dogs," Christy said wistfully. She wished she knew as much. She felt like she'd let Lucky down so badly, losing him in the woods, even if Mom had said it wasn't her fault.

Jake smiled at her. "He really missed you, you know. Mickey distracted him last night, but when I woke him up to go outside to do his business before I went to bed, he seemed miserable. And this morning, he just sat in the basket looking lonely—didn't even want any breakfast. He didn't want me, even if I have been a dog-owner for years. He's your puppy."

Christy nodded, watching as Lucky wove in and out of Mickey's legs. Then he stopped suddenly, looking around, as if he were checking that Christy was still there.

She crouched down, and he raced over to lick her hand quickly before going back to his game.

"See?" Jake nodded at Christy. "Your dog."

Christy smiled. It was true. And she was going to make sure she never lost him again.

Dad had called home to let Mom and Anna know that they'd found Lucky, so Christy wasn't that surprised to find Anna in the front yard waiting for them. She was standing on the bottom of the gate, peering over the top, and she waved madly as soon as she saw the car.

For once, Dad had let Christy hold Lucky on her lap instead of putting him in his travel crate. Every so often, as they drove along, he turned and looked up at her, as though to check that she was still there, and he kept giving her hands loving little licks.

"Lucky, Lucky!" Anna flung open the gate, and rushed over to them, with Mom chasing after her.

"Oh, Christy, I'm so glad you've got him back," Mom said, smiling through the car window.

Christy got out of the car, and Lucky licked Anna, very gently. He could see that the white patch on her face meant he had to be careful.

"Good boy," Christy whispered. She went in through the gate, expecting Lucky to jump down and race around the yard, like he usually did. But this time he stayed snuggled in Christy's arms.

There was nowhere else he would rather be.

HOLLY WEBB

Holly Webb started out as a children's book editor, and wrote her first series for the publisher she worked for. She has been writing ever since, with more than 100 books to her name. Holly lives in England with her husband and three young sons. She has three pet cats, who are always nosing around when Holly is trying to type on her laptop.

For more information about Holly Webb visit:

www.holly-webb.com
www.tigertalesbooks.com